JENNIFER

© ILLUMINATIONS 1982

Jennifer

THE CROCODILE UNDER
LOUIS FINNEBERG'S BED

Illustrated by Nancy Winslow Parker

Written and illustrated by Nancy Winslow Parker

THE CROCODILE UNDER LOUIS FINNEBERG'S BED

Written and illustrated by **Nancy Winslow Parker**

DODD, MEAD & COMPANY / New York

Grateful acknowledgment is made to Lewis Finneburgh for permission to use his name, to Wilbur, his caiman, for permission to publish events in his life, and to Mary O'Connor for permission to use her name.

1   2   3   4   5   6   7   8   9   10

Library of Congress Cataloging in Publication Data
Parker, Nancy Winslow.
    The crocodile under Louis Finneberg's bed.
    SUMMARY: When his pet crocodile grows too large to fit under
his bed, Louis' mother tells him he can no longer keep it.
    [1. Crocodiles—Fiction.   2. Pets—Fiction]
I. Title.
PZ7.P2274Cr   [E]   77-16875
ISBN 0-396-07542-8

To
Laurie Stone
Parker

Talking Crocodile Given to Local Zoological Gardens

SOUTHAMPTON, LONG ISLAND, May 30, 1913—
Judge and Mrs. Julius K. Finneberg and family, promi-
nent members of this town, have given a talking crocodile
to the Zoological Gardens in memory of their son, Louis
K. Finneberg, who mysteriously disappeared over a fort-
night ago.

The crocodile, a rare *Crocodilus niloticus,* eight feet long from tip of nose to tip of tail, had been sent to Louis Finneberg by the boy's grandparents, Colonel and Mrs. Phineas Finneberg, who had been visiting in Egypt as guests of the khedive.

The crocodile, according to Miss Mary O'Connor, a chambermaid in the Finneberg cottage on Dune Road, was immediately drawn to the young Finneberg. It slept under the lad's bed,

bathed in his bathtub,

and shared suppers at the children's dinner table.

With the great care lavished upon the crocodile by the boy, and nourished by the wholesome meals served in the Finneberg home, it grew to full size, with glistening, scaly skin and large, evenly spaced teeth.

Louis Finneberg and the crocodile were inseparable companions. They went to picnics at Rose's Grove,

fishing at the trout pond,

and kite-flying at the Meadow Club.

Every summer they marched in the Fourth of July parade.

Miss O'Connor further stated that Mrs. Finneberg, the former Glorabelle Vandertrack the railroad heiress, insisted the crocodile be disposed of when it grew too large to fit under Louis Finneberg's bed.

It was at this time that the young Finneberg disappeared.

Quite unaccountably, the crocodile began speaking and showed no sorrow at the loss of its devoted master and companion.

The bereaved family continue to search for their missing son and have offered a reward for information leading to his return.

Visiting hours to see the crocodile are from ten to five Tuesday through Sunday, in the Reptile House at the Zoological Gardens. The zoo is closed on Monday. Zoo officials report that vast numbers of people have visited the crocodile and are amazed at its ability to speak and fly kites.

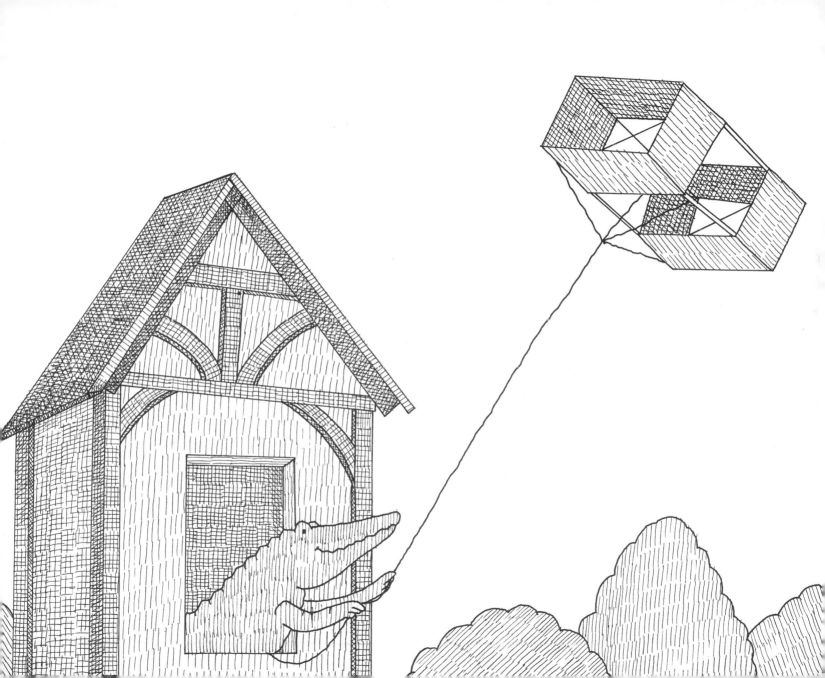

Zoological Gardens Return Talking Crocodile to Donor

SOUTHAMPTON, LONG ISLAND, September 2, 1913—Judge and Mrs. Julius K. Finneberg and family have taken back the talking crocodile they donated to the zoo several months ago, after the mysterious disappearance of their son, Louis K. Finneberg. The zoo superintendent was unable to explain the Finneberg action.

However, Miss Mary O'Connor, a chambermaid in the Finneberg cottage on Dune Road, said that the family had become so attached to the crocodile and its peculiar voice and habits that they could not live without its company. Mrs. Finneberg was so overcome by emotion that she was unable to be interviewed.

Miss O'Connor further stated that the crocodile would once again share suppers at the children's table and sleep under Louis Finneberg's bed.